I0716840

High heels, broken hearts,

and antidepressants

Natalie Pockett

For the girl who first decided that she
wanted to write when she grew up

I haven't quite managed the growing
up part yet, but I've sure been writing

Contents

Growing up

It always happens too fast

Like Riding a Bike

I don't remember learning to ride a bike,
it feels like I grew out of training wheels overnight
and taught myself; swerving on gravel trails
weaving through campsites
chasing my cousins with the wind in my hair.
I was happy then.

One cousin and I are the same age
but somehow he was allowed to grow up faster
When the family was together
he would be up at the fire
and I would be sent to bed.
I don't know who decided that ten-year-old boys
and ten-year-old girls had different bedtimes,
but it wasn't fair.

So my bike was important to me because
we were the same when we played
I wasn't the little girl when I raced down the street
and skidded around corners
I could go just as fast and just as far.

But then he learned how to ride with one hand
so I taught myself how to do it too
and I felt unbalanced but I refused to lose.
If I let them see my fear
I would be just the little girl again.

But then he learned how to ride with no hands
so I tried to do it too,
but it's hard to learn on uneven ground
and I ran over a rock
and I fell.
And I cried.
And just like that, I was the little girl again.

After that, my bike retired to the shed
my cousin didn't want to play as much
I know it's because he wanted to ride his bike
and I was too afraid to ride mine,
but it felt like it was really because he saw
that I was just a little girl.
And little girls don't make good playmates for
ten-year-old boys.

That was a long time ago.
I'm not the little girl anymore
I haven't been in years
but I still don't ride my bike
I've tried but all I can think of
is the rock
and the fall
and the tears.

My Constant

My parents understood how to survive
car rides with three kids in the back seat.
At least one of us on the brink of tears
my dad sings Christmas carols,
my mom pops in a CD,
and we get there without a fight.

When I was little I could never speak in class
my voice was too shaky.
I'd get all warm and pace,
forget what I meant to say,
but I put on a teacup costume
and sang my little heart out on stage.

I've never been able to make friends
but something changes when
we sit together and play.
It's just ink on a page,
but we make it more and
unintentionally create a community.

So now when I don't want to wake up
I force myself out of bed
We have rehearsal, people depend on me
I don't want the younger ones to know
how hard it was to get there.
We'll just play and I'll feel better.

I haven't lived very long
but I've had a lot of life in that time.
I've overcome so much,
I am still working to beat some
but I know I will
with my only true constant.

High heels

My first pair of heels
were pink and plastic.
Filled with sparkles,
a portrait of Aurora over my toes,
stuck on a jelly band
that held my tiny foot in place.

My first pair of heels
were only an inch tall,
but an inch feels like a lot
when you are still waiting to grow.

My first pair of heels
were kept in the dress-up box.
Sitting on a bundle
of princess dresses
and pirate costumes
and magic fairy wands.

My first pair of heels
made me feel beautiful.

My latest pair of heels
are matte gold and strappy.
They shine just a little
when the light is right
and when my dress moves
up and out of the way.

My latest pair of heels
are the tallest I've ever worn
but I still feel small when I wear them
even when my back is straight.

My latest pair of heels
also live in a box.
A shoe box in my closet
where they wait for the event
that will finally give them a chance.

My latest pair of heels
make me feel entirely too grown up.

When I wore my first pair of heels
I would pretend to be walking a runway.
I was a magical princess-model
and the world was my stage.

When I wear my latest pair of heels
I'll have to work not to trip
as I walk across the stage
in a gown that's not mine
and move from childhood
to whatever comes next.

Stranger danger

It was important to have an Instagram
in the sixth grade.
To like all the photos
and be in the class group chats
so that you didn't miss the jokes
at school the next day.
So that you could text the boys
that you liked and the ones you didn't;
It didn't matter as long as you were
texting boys.

I was twelve years old
the first time I got a message
from an account that I didn't recognize
> *Hey! I was scrolling and found your profile*
> *so cute, I have to admit I couldn't resist*
> *clicking on your profile.*
I was polite, I knew about 'stranger danger'
but I had never been called cute by a boy
– a much older boy –
soon he was asking where I lived.

I was sixteen years old
when I got a message saying
        You really have a nice profile with beautiful
        pictures… I hope you are not angry I sent you
        a message
He said that he wanted to be friends
but I knew better by then.
I asked him if that line usually worked
        I don't get what you are saying…
        I just want us to be friends….

Sometime between those two
I started getting different messages
without false promises of friendship.
One man offered me a six-figure salary
and I joked with my friends
that I should have taken it,
because if we don't make it funny
we will just be afraid.

I don't get the nice messages anymore
and I only get offers once in a while,
but every time I open a message request
I still feel my heartbeat drop to my stomach
and I hope that maybe it's just a mistake
and maybe it won't be a man trying to find me.

Love

I pride myself on my ability to translate thoughts to page.
It isn't usually this hard
to fit my life into a template
a theme
a poem that is built to be shared
and that isn't hard to write.
They say to write what you know,
but what if I don't know?

There's a lot of things in this world
that I just don't understand
and maybe I never will,
but I prefer to believe that one day I'll
know what it means to love.
To be in love.

When I was trying to write this,
I came up with a list of things that I love
in an attempt to find a topic.
So, I love my parents, my siblings, and my dogs.
Certain foods, music, books, and Criminal Minds.
Sleep, solitude, quiet, drinks, pills,
and just like that
this doesn't seem like a poem about love anymore.

I am afraid of a lot of things.
Mainly spiders, bears, snakes, heights,
dying alone, and falling in love.
It's strange, isn't it?
A person can be both afraid of
loneliness and the thing that can fix loneliness,
but here I am.

Most of those can be considered rational.
Spiders, bears, and snakes can kill you.
Maybe not here, but somewhere at least.
And you can't fall unless you are at a height
and I really don't like the feeling of falling.
And dying alone is a valid fear,
we are social creatures.
That's why the love thing doesn't make sense.

I like to think that I'll grow out of the fears
but time only seems to make them stronger
and I don't know how to fix it.
I usually know how to fix things.

Maybe love is just something
that I won't understand
until I am in it.
And maybe it will just happen to me.
I hope it happens to me, even if
it is absolutely terrifying.
Because I see my friends,
and my dad,
and a large portion of the population,
and I see that they are happy.
Love did that.

I don't know what I'm trying to say
other than I am ready.
And I really don't like the feeling of falling,
but maybe I'll like the feeling of falling in love.

Love from top to bottom

The first time it happened, at least

Sun, moon, and stars

They say you have to love yourself
before you can love another.

But that can't be right,
he's already becoming my sun, moon, and stars.

Love is like a box of chocolates

Falling in love is like falling asleep,
you don't see it happen until it's done.
Falling in love is like jumping from high
into the calm, safe waters waiting down
below you. It's like eating good food when
the pain of hunger is urging you to.
Falling in love is the most natural,
yet unpredictable feeling there is.
Being in love is like lying under
the warm, spring sun when it doesn't yet burn.
It's like warm apple cider in the cold,
like drifting over calm, quiet waters,
like finding the puzzle piece that fell down
to the floor. Love is always surprising,
yet also familiar. Love is like
a box of chocolates, if it has only
the flavours that you like. Love is hearing
the birds sing in the morning after they
have been away for too many cold months.
Love is feeling your sound disappear and
fit into the music surrounding you.
Love is the most wonderful, yet scary
adventure that humankind can observe.
It is the best gift that we can bestow;
we spend our lives trying to deserve it.

A ballad of song and mourning

In a little town
By the windy shore
Was a lonely young girl
And a charming boy

Every day she walked among the willows
And she sang to the flowers and the bees
And she didn't notice behind her
The boy hiding closely in the trees

He would follow her forever
If she walked all that way
And he would listen to her singing
Until his hearing faded away

And when the snow started to fall
He thought she'd stay home in the warmth
But he saw her footsteps heading
To the forest in the north

He found a place below the willows
A bed of freshly fallen snow
From nearby he heard her singing
He didn't realize that she'd know

He heard soft footsteps coming closer
Felt a strange shift in the air
The snow moved as she settled
Under the willow they would share

She sang softly in his ear
Under the willow tree
And he quietly drifted off to sleep
As he heard her lilting melody

When the cold wind blows
The leaves flying in the breeze
I will lay with you my darling
Under cover of the trees

If the cold wind comes in the summertime
And the clouds cover up the sun
I will shine my light upon you
I'd do it all for the one

The one who holds me when I'm cold
Who rocks me when it's loud
The boy who's always by my side
Forever and ever is our vow

I want you to love me forever
I'll love you longer than that
I will be your very first love
And you will be my very last

When he woke the next morning
Below the willow they had shared
He felt for her beside him
But the snow had been bared

Every day since she left him
He found himself back in the spot
That she had shared herself with him
But his quest came to nought

Many suns and many moons
Watched him lying on the ground
As the seasons changed around him
And the girl was never found

After years were spent just waiting
He found another that stole his heart
And the girl under the willow
Faded away part by part

And as his hair greyly faded
And his kids grew tall and wise
He was watched by another
By the lonely girl's sad eyes

Decades passed and he grew frailer
But she stayed all the same
He lived full of love and laughter
She watched him move to his grave

And when he lay on his deathbed
She couldn't hold back anymore
She lay beside him and she held him
She sang a song for him once more

When the cold wind blows
The leaves flying in the breeze
I will lay with you my darling
Under cover of the trees

If the cold wind comes in the summertime
And the clouds cover up the sun
I will shine my light upon you
I'd do it all for the one

The one who held me when I was cold
Who rocked me gently when it was loud
The boy I wanted by my side
But forever was not our vow

I wish you could have loved me forever
I've loved you even longer than that
I was your very first love
And you have stayed my very last

As you make your way
To your next home in the sky
I will let you go without me
As I have let you live your life

As he took his very last breaths
And felt the girl he had once known
She held his hand as it grew colder
And felt her heart grow cold as stone

Once he was gone she felt a darkness
But she wouldn't let it win
She left the little town behind her
And never returned to where he'd been

Alone was not new to her
She'd been that way her whole life
And she would stay like that forever
No matter how she wished, she would never be a wife

She found a new forest to wander
And she wrote a brand new song
Her solitude may be forced
But she thought sadness would be wrong

It is hard to live forever
When your loved ones have to go
But her heart always remembered
The boy that lay with her in the snow

Falling out of love

It's a long fall
into love.

From strangers,
        to friends,
                to completely in love.

But the fall out of it
that's the dangerous one.

From strangers,
        to friends,
                to completely in love,
                        to unhappily together,
to strangers all over again.

Sun, moon, and stars: part 2

I guess you do have to love yourself
before you can love another.

He was my sun, moon, and stars,
it's called codependency.

Seven

On the first date
that you didn't know was a date,
was the first time I let myself
imagine a future.

On the second date,
we spent all night talking.
I wanted to dance,
but being with you was enough.

In the first month,
we spent all our time together.
That was when I fell in love
and we started to plan forever.

In the second month,
almost everything was the same
only better. More time together,
closer together, happier together.

In the third month,
things started to change.
Not with us, but with everything else.
We were too in love to falter.

In the fourth month
we had so many plans.
Marriage, kids, growing old together,
Germany.

In the fifth month,
everything went wrong.
Not with us, with me.
I didn't want to live any longer.

In the sixth month
I got better, but we got worse.
You didn't change, I did.
I guess that was the problem.

In the seventh month
I couldn't do it anymore.
I couldn't pretend anymore.
I couldn't love you anymore.

We didn't even make it a full seven months
when I had to tell you the truth
and I had to end it there.

I'm sorry

I'm sorry for being what you wanted,
for pretending to be at least.
For lying when you asked if I was happy,
for telling you the truth the next day.
I'm sorry for wrecking all of your plans
but you wrecked mine first
I just never told you,
I morphed my dreams to fit you inside of them.
I'm sorry I didn't say anything earlier.
Maybe if I had just spoken my mind
from the very beginning
you would never have fallen in love
with the girl you thought I wanted to be.
I'm sorry I wasn't that girl
and I'm sorry that I don't want to be anymore.

Why don't you hate me?

Yesterday I thought you would hate me
I expected to never see you again.
Today you say you love me,
you seem sure we'll get back together.
I broke your heart once, I don't want to do it again,
but with the way you're talking, I think I'll have to.
I don't know what to do,
I don't know what to think.
I kind of wish you hated me.

Broken hearts

We broke up yesterday,
this is my fifth poem today.
I guess poetry is for the brokenhearted.
I didn't used to think so.

Patterns

Mostly of grief and spirals

False promises of a fresh start

The celebration starts when we wake.
Family brunch, usually waffles
with sickly sweet strawberries,
blueberries that I never touch,
and a nearly empty can of whipped cream.

We play games together.
Uno, Skip-Bo, Monopoly
but only when Mom has to stop playing.
She's never liked Monopoly.
Not like us.

And when we get tired
of each other's company
we escape to our rooms.
And Mom starts to make food.

Mozza sticks, potato skins,
bacon-wrapped wieners, chips and dip,
and dill pickle cheese ball.
A new dish every hour
to keep us fed and awake.

Later, we're bundled up
on the couch for a movie marathon.
I'm between Mom and Julia,
Ben is on the end.
I can barely keep my eyes open.

Mom makes more food,
and brings out the fake wine.
It's just sparkling juice
but we always insist on using wine glasses
to make ourselves feel older.

I sip on the juice
and we talk about resolutions
 I want to read more
 I want to give more
 I want to do better at school
 I want to spend more time with friends
That's what I say at least.
 I want to be happy
is what I should be saying.

I get my hopes up
as we watch the countdown on TV
and sip the ends of our glasses.
 5 I take a breath
  4 I grip my glass
   3 I sip my drink
    2 I close my eyes
     1 *Happy New Year!* I say

We clink our glasses together
and take one last sip.
I hear fireworks somewhere outside
to me, it sounds like gunshots.
Like a bad omen.

I send out far too many texts
with far too many emojis
and more exclamation points
than I've ever used in my life.
I go to bed first.

I want to be happy
I think.
But how can this year be any better
when it starts the same as all the others?
With false promises and happy texts.

For depression

There is a hole in my head, it is your space.
A constant presence in my spinning mind
the only one that's always by my side.
You hold me in your cold and tight embrace.
I feel you squeeze the soul out of my hands
and the happiness from my lonely heart.
I can't recall a time we were apart
from one another. No one understands
the bond that we share or my connection
to your malicious presence. I am not
whole without you, or maybe I've forgot
I can survive without the direction
of your intentions that push to the dark,
that tell me over again I cannot.

For venlafaxine

You are the one that holds my demons back,
that shines a light upon my spinning mind,
my consciousness and your work so entwined
the gap between the two of us a crack
so small I can never know what is me.
You colour my reality with more
nice serotonin than I ever saw.
I can't survive without you and your glee,
your chemicals are what bring me each dawn.
I cannot handle your dizzying lack
of presence, my universe out of whack.
If I had been told my body would mourn
the lack of small capsules of pink and black
I never would have thought that I'd be glad.

Anti-hero

If my life were a TV show
I wouldn't be the hero.
I wouldn't even be the main character,
I don't think so at least
and that's what matters in the end.
Who cares how many people
root for you,
if in your own head
you're at worst the villain
and at best the anti-hero?

Fourteen hours from home

I was not raised in excess.
Just enough for us and a little left to share,
money always tight but never lacking.
Homeowners, but not without a struggle,
the pantry not quite full but not empty either.
Just hovering somewhere around good enough.

I have three parents.
An accountant and a CSO and a hairdresser and
a teacher and a musician and
a town councillor and a bartender
And how is it that I have three parents but they have seven jobs?
And how is it that we are not covered in riches,
when we average over two careers per adult?

Then the bills come in
And this week's groceries cost two hundred dollars
But it's only two bags of food
And how are two bags of food going to feed six people for a week?
And how is it that we can only afford two bags of food?
With my dad working fourteen-hour days
we should have more than this.

I can't understand how people are still going,
still tolerating the work and the lack of reward,
but then I look at my life.
Leaving my house at seven o'clock in the morning,
not home until after nine.
A nine-hour school day followed by four hours of training
for a job that doesn't yet pay me.

The system's smart,
it starts our training early
so that when I'm forty-eight
and working three jobs to feed my kids
I won't be surprised.
It'll be normal;
people don't object to normal.

They especially don't object to normal
when they don't have enough energy to do anything
but eat and sleep
and do it all again the very next day.

I love you so much more

I remember painting in your basement,
you hung up every picture I gave you,
taught me to sign my work just like a real artist.
Even before I could colour in the lines,
you always told me they were beautiful.

I remember coming to your place,
and finding you waiting on the deck.
I remember how your house smelled,
it smelled like you
and it smelled like fresh banana muffins.
You always baked them fresh for me.

I remember that I got sick one time,
so I came to your house for the day,
just me.
I remember sitting in the comfy armchair,
curled up under a mountain of blankets.
I watched game shows on your old TV,
and I listened to the trains through the screen door,
and I listened to you in the kitchen behind me.
You kept checking to see that I was okay.

I remember the first time that I really knew you were getting older.
We came over for a garage sale,
it was time to sell your house.
I remember how the tables filled your driveway,
how they were covered in everything that reminded me of you.
I remember saying goodbye to the house,
to your garden,
to your art studio in the basement,
and to the kitchen that smelt a little too much like home.

I remember when you stopped dying your hair,
letting the red that I had always known
fade to the grey that I would remember.
You looked so beautiful,
it just wasn't the same as how it had always been.

I remember the first time you forgot my name.
I already knew that you were starting to have trouble remembering,
but you had always remembered me.
I remember holding in the tears while I smiled and reminded you.
And I remember how the tears came flooding out that night,
the moment that I was alone.

I remember the first time I visited you in the hospital.
I think that you had fallen,
it didn't matter.
You were going to be okay,
you told me so.
I left with a smile on my face,
you were going home soon.

Today, when I visited you in the hospital,
you didn't tell me you were going to be okay.
You asked me the same questions that I answered yesterday.
You showed me your nails,
I don't know if you remember that I painted them.
You introduced me to the doctor,
you still don't remember my name.
I left with tears welling up,
you aren't going home soon.

A while back, I visited on a good day.
You remembered me,
and just before I left, you looked right at me and said:
"I am so proud of you."
I don't know why you said that,
maybe you knew that I needed to hear it.
You can't always figure out who I am,
but you're still proud of me.
I told you I loved you as I left,
you told me:
"I love you so much more."

You have watched me grow for my whole life,
now I have to watch you fade for the rest of yours.
And every time I picture you all that I can think is
please don't make me watch you die.
I mumble quiet prayers,
please don't make me watch her die,
I haven't had her long enough,
please just give me one more chance,
let me tell her that it's okay,
and that I love her so much more.

I will be okay

Depression is a stalker.
You don't know he's there,
that he's just behind you,
watching,
      waiting,
            learning your weaknesses
until it's too late and he's in your house.

Depression is a fire.
Its existence was never intended,
but now it is undeniable,
it's everywhere,
      smothering you with every breath
until it burns too much to breathe,
and you can do nothing but lay in the heat.

Depression is an acting exercise.
If they don't know how bad it is, you're doing it right,
you were never a peppy child
      I was so tired of pretending to be one
you just have a low baseline
      'suicidal' is an emergency, not a baseline
you need to push through
      what do you think I've been doing?
And you file the thoughts back
into the deepest folds of your mind.

Depression is sinking,
not everyone who drowns can't swim.
The water looked so refreshing
until I got too tired to float,
          too tired to cope.
I felt the weightlessness dissipate,
the waters began to rise,
and before I knew it, I was too deep to swim back to shore.

If depression is a stalker,
          a fire,
                    an acting exercise,
                              sinking
Support is an arrest,
          a firetruck,
                    a scene-break,
                              a lifeguard,
I say that I don't want to talk,
          I love that you offer though,
I say that I am okay,
          I believe that someday I will be.
I act annoyed when you look at me with concern
because you've seen through the front,
but I know that if I sink too far,
you will pull me back to the surface.

If depression is a hand grenade thrown into my life,
a friend is the hope that it will be the last.
They are the force that pulls me out of the rubble,
and the hand that helps me to rebuild.

www.ingramcontent.com/pod-product-compliance
Lightning Source LLC
Chambersburg PA
CBHW030908200726
48289CB00003B/939